Little Red Riding Hood

PUFFIN BOOKS
Published by the Penguin Group
Penguin Putnam Books for Young Readers,
345 Hudson Street, New York, New York 10014, U.S.A.
Penguin Books Ltd, 27 Wrights Lane, London W8 5TZ, England
Penguin Books Australia Ltd, Ringwood, Victoria, Australia
Penguin Books Canada Ltd, 10 Alcorn Avenue, Toronto, Ontario, Canada M4V 3B2
Penguin Books (N.Z.) Ltd, 182-190 Wairau Road, Auckland 10, New Zealand

Penguin Books Ltd, Registered Offices: Harmondsworth, Middlesex, England

First published by Viking and Puffin Books,
members of Penguin Putnam Books for Young Readers, 2000

7 9 10 8 6

LIBRARY OF CONGRESS CATALOGING-IN-PUBLICATION DATA:
Ziefert, Harriet.
Little Red Riding Hood / by Harriet Ziefert ; illustrated by Emily Bolam.
p. cm. — (A Viking easy-to-read classic)
Summary: A little girl meets a hungry wolf in the forest
while on her way to visit her grandmother.
ISBN 0-670-88389-1 (hardcover).—ISBN 0-14-056529-9 (pbk).
[1. Fairy tales. 2. Folklore—Germany.] I. Bolam, Emily, ill.
II. Little Red Riding Hood. English. III. Title. IV. Series.
PZ8.Z154Li 2000 398.2'0943'02 [E]—DC21 99-23210 CIP

Printed in China
Set in Bookman

Reading Level 1.9

Little Red Riding Hood

retold by Harriet Ziefert
illustrated by Emily Bolam

PUFFIN BOOKS

Little Red Riding Hood
lived with her mother
in a little house
near the woods.

One day her mother said,
"Your grandmother is sick.
These cakes will make
her feel better.
Will you take them to her?"

"I will," said Little Red Riding Hood.

“Be careful,” said her mother.
“Don’t talk to any strangers
on the way.”

“I will be careful,” said
Little Red Riding Hood.
“I will not talk to strangers.”

Little Red Riding Hood
waved to a woodcutter.
Then she met a wolf.

"Good morning,"
said the wolf.
"Where are you going?"

"I'm taking cakes
to my grandmother.
She is sick."

"Why don't you take her
some flowers, too?"
said the wolf.

"What a good idea!" said
Little Red Riding Hood.

Little Red Riding Hood
picked some flowers.
And the wolf ran off to
Grandma's house.

“Who is there?”
asked Grandma.

“It’s me—it’s
Little Red Riding Hood,”
said the wolf in a high voice.

“Come in, my dear,”
said Grandma.

The wolf went right to
Grandma’s bedroom.

And he had himself
a very good meal.

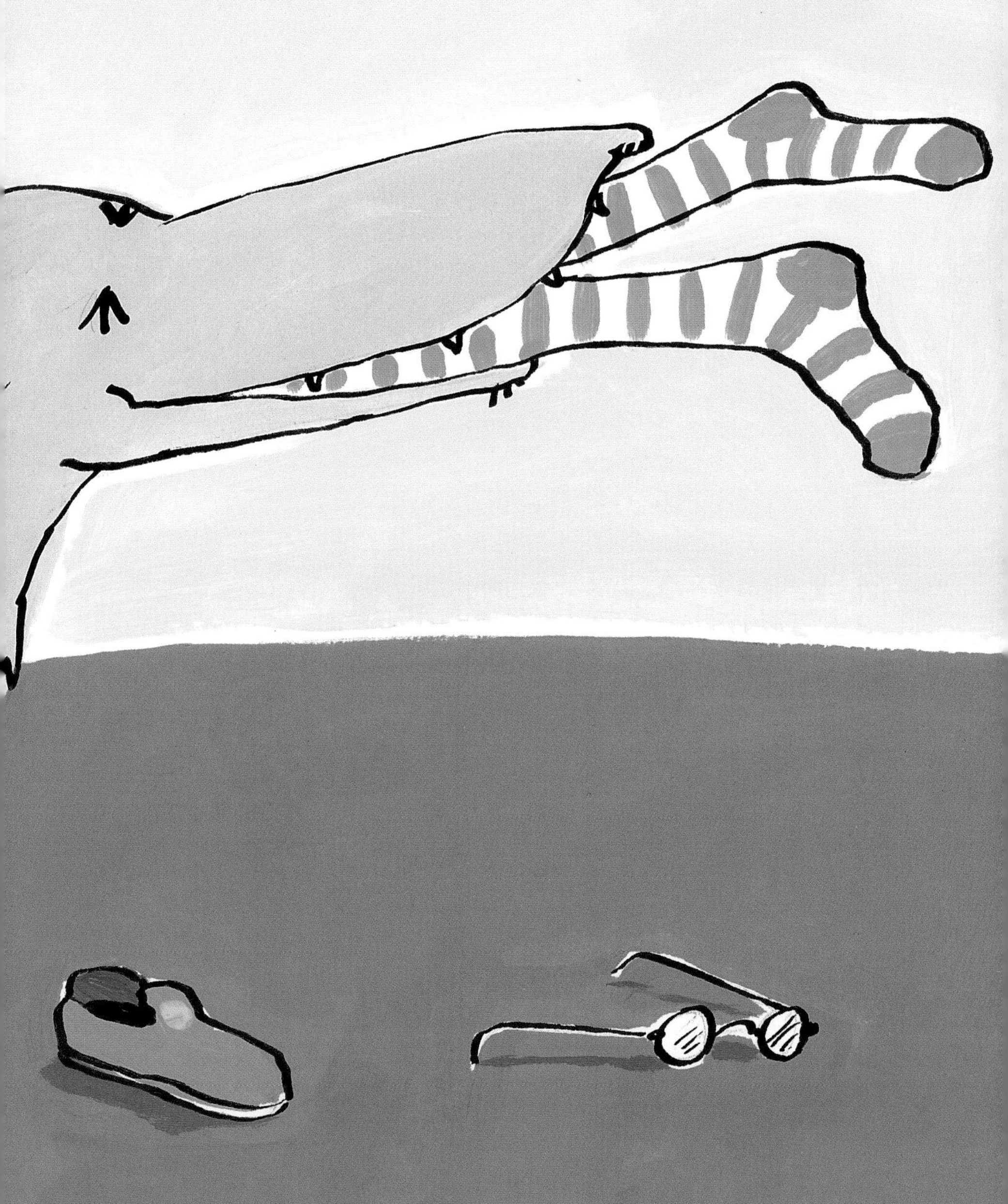

The wolf waited for
Little Red Riding Hood.

Before long, he heard
a knock at the door.

"Come in, my dear,"
said the wolf.

Little Red Riding Hood said,
"Oh, Grandma—what big eyes
you have."

“The better to see you with,
my dear,” said the wolf.

"Oh, Grandma—what big ears you have," said Little Red Riding Hood.

"The better to hear you with, my dear," said the wolf.

“Oh, Grandma—what big teeth you have,” said Little Red Riding Hood.

"The better to EAT you with,
my dear!" said the wolf.

“You’re not my grandma,”
said Little Red Riding Hood.
But it was too late.

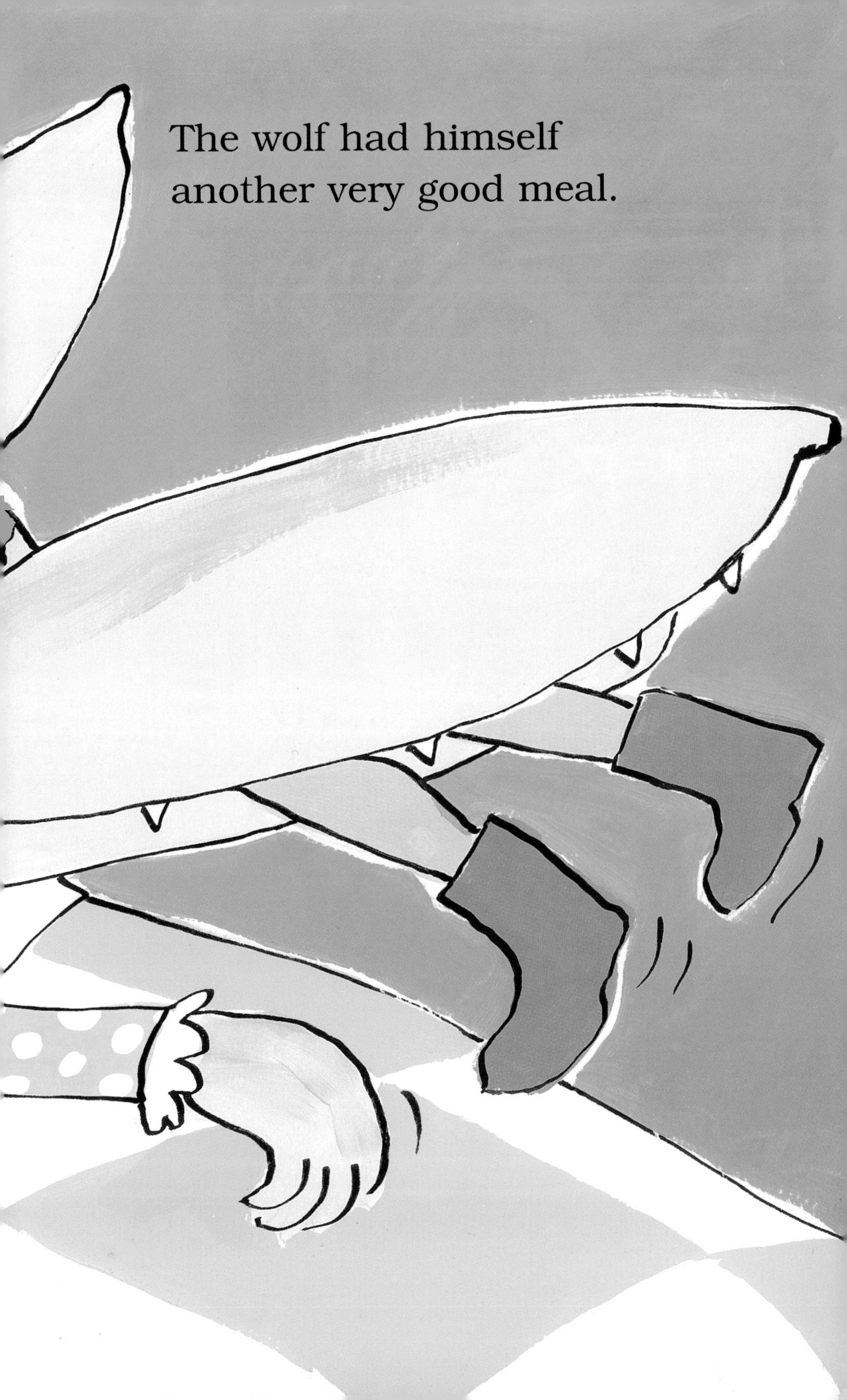

The wolf had himself
another very good meal.

The woodcutter saw the open door
and went inside.

As soon as he saw the wolf,
he lifted his ax and . . .

killed the wolf.

Little Red Riding Hood
and her grandmother
stepped out.

From that day on,
Little Red Riding Hood
never, ever talked to
strangers again.